Poetic POLLY

ORCHARD BOOKS

Carmelite House, 50 Victoria Embankment, London EC4Y 0DZ

Orchard Books Australia

Level 17/207 Kent Street, Sydney, NSW 2000

First published in 1998 under the title
POLLY THE MOST POETIC PERSON by Orchard Books
This updated version published in 2015

ISBN: 978 1 40833 754 7

Text © Laurence Anholt 2015
Illustrations © Tony Ross 1998

The rights of Laurence Anholt to be identified as the author and Tony
Ross to be identified as the illustrator of this work have been asserted by
them in accordance with the Copyright, Designs and Patents Act, 1988.

A CIP catalogue record for this book is available
from the British Library.

1 3 5 7 9 10 8 6 4 2

Printed and bound by CPI Group (UK) Ltd, Croydon, CR0 4YY

The paper and board used in this book are made from wood
from responsible sources.

Orchard Books is an imprint of Hachette Children's Group and published by
the Watts Publishing Group Limited, an Hachette UK company.

www.hachette.co.uk

Poetic POLLY

Laurence Anholt

Illustrated by Tony Ross

ORCHARD

www.anholt.co.uk

Hee, hee, hello everyone!
My name is **Ruby** and I have the
funniest family in the world.
In these books, I will introduce you
to my **freaky family**.

You will meet people like…

Tiny Tina

Bendy Ben

Mucky Micky

Brainy Boris

Brave Bruno

Hairy Harold

But this book is all about … my
poetic auntie, **POLLY**.

We are going to meet my auntie, Polly, the most poetic person on the whole planet. No matter how she tries, Polly can't stop making poems.

As soon as Polly wakes up in the morning, she starts to rhyme... "Poems in the bedroom, poems in the shower, poems in the kitchen, hour after hour.

When I have my breakfast, or
when I flush the loo, I like poems
all the time, with everything I do."

Auntie Polly loved her poems.
But her friends began to get cross.
"Please, Polly, no more poems!"
they said.

"But to rhyme all the time
isn't a crime."

Polly tried to get a job, but no one wanted a poet in a supermarket. "Mustard, custard, carrots, peas. Thank you, Madam, five pounds please."

Auntie Polly tried to get a job in a school. But no one wanted a rhyming lollipop lady.

"Hurry, children, don't delay, a great big lorry is coming this way."

Auntie Polly tried to get a job in the police force. But no one wanted a poetic policewoman.

"Stop! Stop! You naughty pest,
drop that loot. You're under
arrest."

So Auntie Polly sat at home all
alone... "No one wants me, it
makes me sad. People think my
poems are bad."

Polly was a lonely poet. But she couldn't stop rhyming. At last, Polly went to see a clever doctor.

The doctor's name was Doctor Bill.
"Doctor Bill, will you give
me a pill?
I can't stop rhyming.
It's making me ill."

Doctor Bill looked inside Polly's
mouth. "Open wide," he said.
"Say, 'Aah'!"
"Aah. Bah. Far. Star. Seven
monkeys in a car."

Then Doctor Bill shone a torch
inside Polly's mouth. "Say, 'Ooh'!"
he said.
"Ooh, too. To-wit to-woo. Nine
owls in a stew."

"Yes," said Doctor Bill. "A bad case of rhyming. I'm afraid there is no cure. I hope no one else will catch it. Next patient, please."

So Auntie Polly started to walk
slowly home. She felt sadder
than ever.

"It's a lonely life, when you're a poet. I've always guessed it - now I know it."

Auntie Polly walked past a big
factory. A sign said: "THE HAPPY
BIRTHDAY CARD FACTORY".

But the people inside the factory were not happy at all. They could make nice birthday cards but they

could not write the poems to go inside them.

"I hope your birthday is full of fun, bright and warm just like the...er... um..."

The people in the factory couldn't rhyme at all. Auntie Polly knocked at the door.

"Knock, knock, excuse me please, I could write your poems with ease."

Auntie Polly had lots of ideas for birthday poems.

Your birthday comes just
once a year
be sure to smile
from ear to ear.

'Happy birthday, darling sister, I like you more than a nasty blister.'

'Granny, your eyes are bright and twinkly. With every year you get more wrinkly.'

'Tomatoes are red and violets are blue, from Polly the poet – happy birthday to you!'

Everyone at the Happy Birthday
Card Factory began to clap.

They thought Auntie Polly was the best poet in the world.

They asked if she would like a job at the Happy Birthday Card Factory.

"Thank you, thank you, I'd
love to stay, and write my poems
every day."

So Polly the poet stayed forever at
the Happy Birthday Card Factory.
And everyone loved her.

Each year Polly sent a special
birthday poem to Doctor Bill.
She was glad he hadn't made
her better.

Doctor Bill liked the cards but he didn't really need the poem. He had too many poems already.

Because Doctor Bill had caught
Polly's rhyming...

"Take one of these, if you cough
or sneeze. You'll soon feel better –
next patient, please!"

THE END

MY
FREAKY
FAMILY

COLLECT THEM ALL!

RUDE RUBY	978 1 40833 639 7
MUCKY MICKY	978 1 40833 764 6
POETIC POLLY	978 1 40833 754 7
BRAINY BORIS	978 1 40833 756 1
BRAVE BRUNO	978 1 40833 762 2
TINY TINA	978 1 40833 760 8
BENDY BEN	978 1 40833 758 5
HAIRY HAROLD	978 1 40833 752 3

Also available as an ebook